Adapted by Meredith Rusu
from the teleplay by Steven Sullivan

Published by Scholastic Inc., *Publishers since 1920.* SCHOLASTIC and associated logos are trademarks and/or registered trademarks of Scholastic Inc.

ISBN 978-1-338-11275-7

10 9 8 7 6 5 4 3 2 1   17 18 19 20 21
40
Printed in the U.S.A.
First printing 2017
Book design by Erin McMahon and Becky James

SCHOLASTIC INC.

It was a bright, sunny morning in Charmville. Hazel was just waking up.

"*Meeeoooow!*" Hazel's cat, Seven, hopped on the bed.

"Let me guess, you'd like some breakfast?" Hazel giggled. "Coming right up!"

Hazel headed to the kitchen. Her mom was there holding a clipboard.

"Good morning, Mom!" said Hazel.

"It's a very good morning," her mom replied. "It's Baby Unicorn Day!"

Hazel gasped. Baby Unicorn Day was the one day each year that new baby unicorns came sliding down the rainbows in the rainbow fields to meet their mommies. It had always sounded so *charmazing*!

"Can Posie, Lavender, and I come?" Hazel asked eagerly.

"Of course!" her mom said with a smile. "You girls would be a great help."

"Sparktastic!" cheered Hazel. "We're going to be baby unicorn wranglers!"

A short while later, the Little Charmers were ready to fly to the rainbow fields. They had even charmed up sparkling unicorn horns to wear for the occasion.

"The rainbow fields are so pretty!" said Posie when they arrived.
"There are rainbows and sparkles . . ."

"And baby unicorns!" Hazel's mom announced, pointing to a
nearby rainbow.

Sure enough, a pink baby unicorn was just sliding down, ready to be caught.

"I've got him!" cried Posie.

Ooof! The baby slid right into Posie's arms and they toppled to the ground.

"Aww! So cute!" said the Little Charmers.

Not far away, the unicorn's mommy was waiting. The tiny baby ran to its mommy and they nuzzled.

"DOUBLE CUTE!" cried the Little Charmers.

One by one, baby
unicorns slid down
the rainbows into the
Charmers' waiting arms.

Each baby's horn flashed bright
and made a magical sound
when it landed: *Brinnnng!*

"Thanks for all your help, girls," said Hazel's mom. "Mind watching these little guys while I go find the rest of the mommies?"

"Of course!" said Hazel. "We'll make sure they're cuddle ready."

Just as Hazel's mom left, *another* baby unicorn slid down the rainbow.

"Gotcha!" cried Hazel. "Always room for one more!"

This baby's mommy was waiting nearby. The baby ran to nuzzle her.

SQUEAK! SQUEAK!

"Huh," said Hazel. "His horn's a squeaker, not a blinker like the others."

"We should call him Squeaker!" cried Posie.

"Don't you think he would like a sparkly, blinking horn like his friends?" Hazel asked.

"He looks pretty happy to me," said Posie.

But Hazel was certain Squeaker would be even *happier* with a sparkly horn.

"Sparkle up, Charmers!"

"Make this baby that's just been born a magically flashing unicorn!"

Poof! The charm hit Squeaker's horn. And then . . .
HOOOOOOONNNN-OOOOOOONNNNK!

Oh, no! Squeaker's horn was glowing, but instead of making a magical sound, it blasted like a foghorn!

All the baby unicorns ran away frightened—even Squeaker!

"Wait, come back!" cried Hazel.

"Don't worry," said Lavender and Posie. "We'll go get the babies while you go after Squeaker!"

Just then, Hazel's mom returned. Hazel told her what had happened.

"I'm really sorry," said Hazel. "I was just trying to help Squeaker fit in."

"Honey, it's okay for Squeaker not to be like all the rest," said her mom. "Our differences are what make us special."

Hazel realized her mom was right. "Squeaker was perfect just the way he was," she said. "Don't worry. I'll find him!"

Hazel searched high and low. Finally, she found the sad baby unicorn hiding in a crystal cave.

"Squeaker, please come out," said Hazel. "Your horn was perfect just the way it was. It was actually what made you so special! And look! There's someone out here who wants to see you!"

Hazel's kind words were like magic. Squeaker came out and nuzzled with his mommy.

"Aw!" said Hazel. "That's triple cute! Come on. Let's get back to the corral."

Hazel and the unicorns returned. But Posie and Lavender still hadn't come back with the other babies.

"It's getting late, and the fog is getting thicker," Hazel's mom said, worried.

"Maybe Squeaker can guide them back through the fog!" exclaimed Hazel.

Squeaker blew his horn as loud as he could.
HOOOOOOONNNNNN-OOOOOONNNNK!

The noise was just what Posie, Lavender, and the babies needed to find their way home. They were safe!

"Squeaker, you're a unicorn hero!" cried Hazel.

Squeak! Squeak! The baby unicorn nuzzled her.

"Hey, the horn spell wore off!" exclaimed Posie. "Squeaker's back to his old self."

Hazel smiled and gave Squeaker a big hug. "Just the way he's supposed to be."